For Andrea & Claudia
— I.F.

For Mom & Dad, who helped
— J.T.

TIGER TALES
an imprint of ME Media LLC
202 Old Ridgefield Road, Wilton, Connecticut 06897
First published in the United States 2001
Originally published in Great Britain 1999 by
Little Tiger Press, London
Text © 1999 Isobel Finn copyright
Illustrations © 1999 Jack Tickle
CIP Data is available • ISBN 1-58925-007-9
First American edition • Printed in China
3 5 7 9 10 8 6 4 2

The Very Lazy Ladybug

by
Isobel Finn

Illustrated by
Jack Tickle

tiger tales

This is the story
of a very lazy ladybug.

and all night.

Because she slept
all day and all night,
this lazy ladybug didn't
know how to fly.

One day the lazy
ladybug wanted to
sleep somewhere else.
But what could she
do if she couldn't fly?

Then the lazy
ladybug had a
very good idea.

she hopped into her pouch.

But the kangaroo liked to

JUMP!

"I can't sleep in here,"
cried the lazy ladybug.
"It's too bumpy."

So when a tiger padded by . . .

But the tiger liked to

ROAR!

"I can't sleep here," said the lazy ladybug. "It's too noisy."

So when a crocodile swam by . . .

she hopped onto his tail.

But the crocodile liked to

SWISH

his tail in the water.

"I can't sleep here,"
said the lazy ladybug.
"I'll fall into the river!"

So when a monkey swung by . . .

she hopped onto her head.

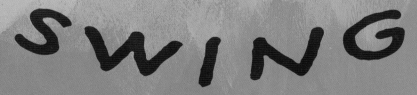

But the monkey liked to

SWING

from branch to branch.

"I can't sleep here," said the lazy ladybug. "I'm feeling dizzy."

So when a bear ambled by . . .

"I can't sleep here," said the lazy ladybug. "He'll never sit still."

So when a tortoise plodded by . . .

she hopped onto her shell.

But the
tortoise liked to
S N O O Z E
in the sun.
"I can't sleep here,"
said the lazy ladybug.
"It's too hot."

So when an elephant walked by . . .

she hopped onto his trunk.

At last, thought the lazy ladybug. I've found someone who doesn't . . .

jump . . .

But at that very moment . . .

the elephant

HOOo

And poor old lazy ladybug . . .

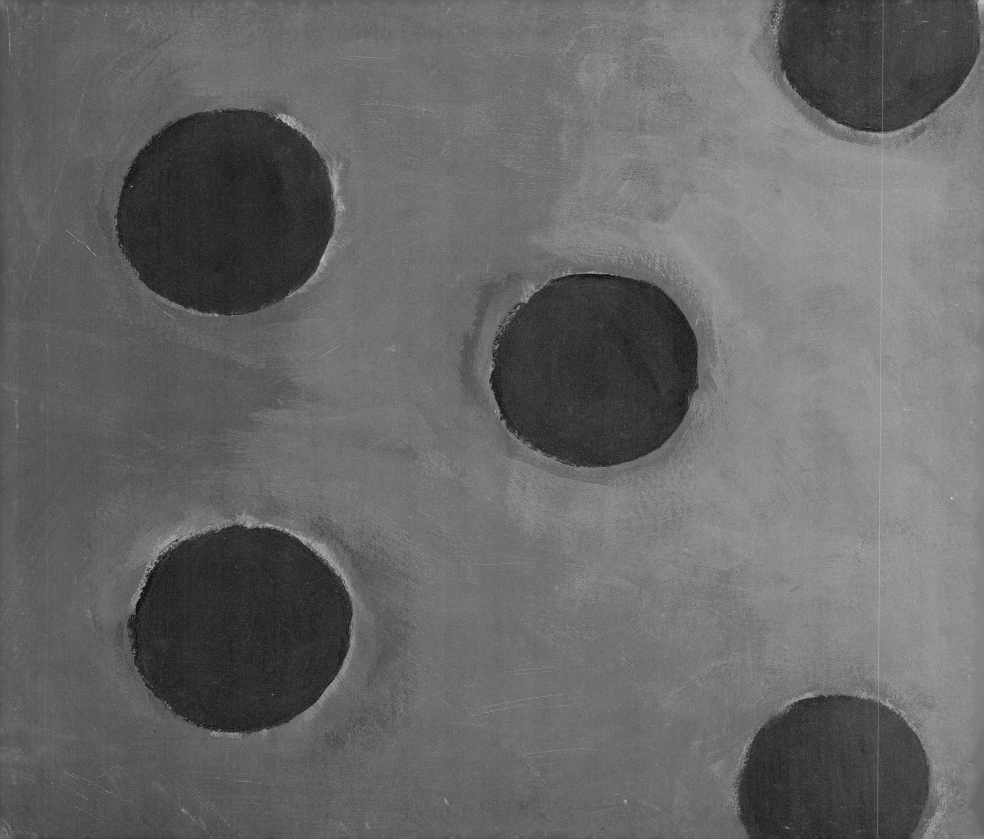